HOW TO SHARE WITH A BEAR

ERIC PINDER

Pictures by STEPHANIE GRAEGIN

Farrar Straus Giroux • New York

One cold day, Thomas gathered
some pillows and blankets and
made a warm, cozy cave.

GUIDE TO BEARS

The cave was too dark to read in,
so Thomas went to get a flashlight.
When he returned, he could hear
something bump and thump and
move around in the cave.

Something big.

Thomas peered inside.
Two shy brown eyes stared back.

It was a bear!

Everyone knows that bears like
berries, so Thomas made a trail
of blueberries leading away from
the cave.

Then he waited.

Sniff. Snort. Snuff.

Soon enough, the bear bumbled through the hall, bustled down the stairs, and disappeared.

Quick as he could, Thomas got his
favorite books and rushed back to
the cave.

Too late!

The bear was already there. Caves
never stay empty for long.

Bears love to scratch their backs
on trees, so Thomas found his mom's
wooden back scratcher, gave himself a
good scratching, then set the scratcher
down outside his bedroom door.

The bear shuffled
out to grab it.

Scritch.
Scrooch.
Scratch.

Thomas crawled into his cave and
started to read, until a floating tuft
of bear fur tickled his nose.

Achoo!

He went to get a tissue.

When he turned around, the bear
was in the cave again.

Bears love to fish in streams,
so Thomas filled the sink and
dropped in some bath toys.

Splish.
Splash.
Splink.

The bear came running.

Thomas barely got comfortable in
his cave before he heard a new noise.

Gurgle. Burble. Plink.

The bear must have turned the water back
on. Thomas went to shut the faucet off.

The bear passed him in the hall.

Bears like honey, so Thomas set out a
bowl of honey oat cereal in the kitchen.
He put on his honeybee costume and said
BZZZZ! as loud as he could.

Then he dashed away flapping his arms,
leading the bear downstairs.

The bear smelled the honey
and stopped to gobble up the
cereal, while Thomas hurried to
his cave. At last he could read!

That's when the bear came back.
When he saw Thomas in the cave,
he tried to snuggle in next to him.
But the cave was too small. The
bear started to cry.

Thomas felt sad for tricking the bear. "You can read, too," he told him. "Come and look." Thomas tried to make more room by pushing out the walls.

CAVE-IN!

Thomas poked his head out. The bear giggled. Thomas grinned. "Let's build a bigger cave," he said. "We can share."

Thomas huddled with the bear in their
big new cave.
They shared a bowl of blueberries.
They shared a good book.

And Thomas learned that bears
like one thing even more than fish
or blueberries or honey.
They like their big brothers.

How to Build a Cave

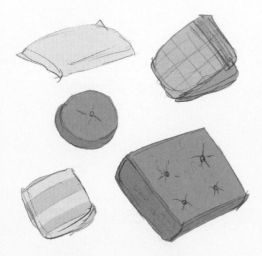

1. Gather all the pillows, cushions, and blankets you can, and bring them to the site of your cave.

2. Use the largest pillows and cushions to construct your walls. Lean them against one another. Use smaller pillows as inside support.

3. Use the blankets and lighter pillows to make your roof.

4. Enjoy your cave!